A BEAR BELONGS
A RESCUE STORY

Catherine Barr

Illustrated by
Harriet Hobday

BLOOMSBURY
CHILDREN'S BOOKS
LONDON OXFORD NEW YORK NEW DELHI SYDNEY

For Dr (Hons) Wong Siew Te for his tireless work saving sun bears
and generous, enthusiastic help with this book – C.B.

For my wonderful students and mentees at
Leith School of Art – H.H.

BLOOMSBURY CHILDREN'S BOOKS
Bloomsbury Publishing Plc
50 Bedford Square, London, WC1B 3DP, UK
Bloomsbury Publishing Ireland Limited
29 Earlsfort Terrace, Dublin 2, D02 AY28, Ireland

BLOOMSBURY, BLOOMSBURY CHILDREN'S BOOKS
and the Diana logo are trademarks of Bloomsbury Publishing Plc

First published in Great Britain 2025 by Bloomsbury Publishing Plc

Consultant: Dr (Hons) Wong Siew Te, CEO and Founder of the Bornean Sun Bear Conservation Centre (BSBCC)

A catalogue record for this book is available from the British Library
ISBN: HB 978-1-5266-5568-4
eBook: 978-1-5266-7410-4

2 4 6 8 10 9 7 5 3 1

Printed and bound in China by Leo Paper Products, Heshan, Guangdong

FSC
www.fsc.org
MIX
Paper | Supporting
responsible forestry
FSC® C020056

To find out more about our authors and books
visit www.bloomsbury.com
and sign up for our newsletters
For product safety related questions contact
productsafety@bloomsbury.com

Contents

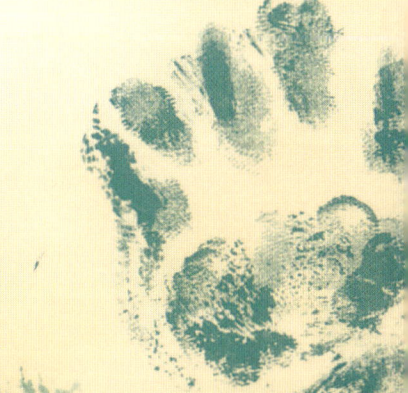

A very rare bear

Bears are in trouble.

From powerful polar bears to shaggy sloth bears and great grizzly bears, each has a different story but they all face similar threats.

And we humans are a bear's biggest threat.

Arctic ice is melting and forest homes are being bulldozed. Tropical forests around the world are being ripped up and even in protected areas, danger lurks.

This threat is greatest in Southeast Asian rainforests. These magical, deep, dark, damp habitats are shrinking. Here, adult bears are poached, which means people hunt bears for their paws and other body parts and sell them to the illegal wildlife trade to be made into trophies or used in traditional medicine.

Mother bears are killed leaving orphaned cubs to be sold illegally as pets.

These forests are home to the smallest and one of the rarest bears of all . . . the sun bear. Sun bears are mysterious and little understood bears. They are extremely rare and one of the most endangered species in the world, which means they are at risk of extinction. They may look cute and cuddly but they are wild and not for petting. They belong deep in the forest, far from humans.

This is the true story of three little bears who were taken from their wild home. It is the story of their rescue and eventually their release back into the rainforest, where sun bears belong.

Part One:

Stolen!

Tan-Tan is tiny. The little cub curls close to her
mother in their leafy forest home. This mother and
her cub are wild sun bears, huddled together in the
tropical rainforest. But soon everything will change.

The hunters have tracked Tan-Tan down. They shoot her
mother and then pull the cub roughly from her mother's
warm black fur. She clutches at the honey-coloured
V-shaped marking like a rising sun on her mother's chest.
Under the cover of darkness, Tan-Tan, only months old,
is stolen from her mother and her home – from all she
has ever known.

She will never see her mother again. But this little
bear will find hope on a new journey ...

The Sun sets on a secret

Tan-Tan is shaking in her crude, cruel cage. She tips and tumbles as her new prison rocks in the back of a truck hurtling far from the lush jungle she is from, full of trees she is not yet old enough to climb.

By dawn, the truck reaches a faraway town. Tan-Tan's poachers look for a good price – after all, she is a very cute bear. But they are careful. They know it is against the law to sell a wild baby bear.

They manage to make a quick sale, then speed off down a dirt track and disappear in a cloud of red dust, taking their secrets with them. Tan-Tan fetched a good price. But the man who bought her has secrets of his own. He bought Tan-Tan in order to rescue her! He phones the local Wildlife Department and together they wait as the Sun sets.

When the Wildlife Department arrive they give her the name 'Tan-Tan' after the tropical town where her rescuer is from. Then they make a desperate call. They ring the best person for saving a sun bear – the world expert on a mission to save sun bears.

His name is Dr Wong.

Three little bears

Dr Wong dreads
news of a captured bear
taken from its wild habitat.
He thinks about his crowded
sanctuary – the Bornean Sun Bear
Conservation Centre – and wonders where
he can squeeze in another little bear.

The Wildlife Department deliver Tan-Tan to
Dr Wong's safety on a hot, humid day. Luckily she is found to be
healthy and well. Here, she will be given every chance to thrive
and return to live in the forest one day.

Soon after, Dr Wong is asked to find room for another two bears. Sun bear cubs Boboi and Kitud have been found trembling together in a pen in a villager's yard where they were kept as pets. Their keeper fed them milk and rice and fish but bears need to eat berries, fruit and honey.

Now Dr Wong has three new little bears looking for love and a home.

Luckily Tan-Tan, Boboi and Kitud soon become friends. This story follows the stolen bear cubs' journey back to their beloved forest.

What makes a sun bear so special?

All sun bears have a V-shape on their chest that gives them their name, as it sometimes looks like the rising or setting Sun. No two marks are the same, but it stands out against their soft black hair. Their satiny coat is short enough to keep them cool but tough enough to protect them from sharp twigs as they scramble up trees. With gangly back legs and slender arms, sun bears are good at climbing. They climb to perch on a branch or rest in a homemade nest.

Also known as honey bears, sun bears love to follow the bees. These agile bears curl their long tongues into beehives to lap up this sweet, high-up treat. Back on the ground these little bears can, unusually for bears, stand up tall on their long back legs.

Tragically, the illegal wildlife trade in bear parts and the destruction of their forest home is pushing sun bears towards extinction. Bornean sun bears are the smallest of all sun bears. Scientists believe this may be because they have smaller territories and less food than others. These littlest of bears are difficult to find and tricky to count but experts say they are in immediate danger.

But there are three little bears whose luck miraculously changed . . .

Meet the bears

Tan-Tan is the smallest of the three bears. But she has a talent that rivals no other – she is a record-breaking climber! Tan-Tan is a fast learner with a sweet, caring nature.

Boboi is happiest when Kitud and Tan-Tan are close. He is like a big brother, always watching out for the other two. Boboi is cheeky and full of energy. He will always find ways to have fun!

Kitud is the gentle, confident leader. She is curious and adventurous and loves eating coconuts. Kitud eats slowly with far better manners than her friend Boboi!

The Bear Care Crew

Three little bears crouch against the cool, safe walls of the Bear House in Dr Wong's Bornean Sun Bear Conservation Centre, safe at last from poachers and rescued from life in a cage. In the wild where they were born, Tan-Tan, Boboi and Kitud would keep close to their mothers who would protect them from biting insects and deadly snakes. Baby bears cuddle for comfort, snuggling in to drink their mother's warm milk.

Here, they are orphans. They hear human footsteps and softly spoken voices. They smell fruit and vegetables being chopped up for their meals and they can also smell other bears.

They are looked after by a team of human volunteers that make up the Bear Care Crew. They cuddle the bears and give them bottled goat's milk to help them grow. Their special bond helps scared little bears feel calm and safe.

Bear check-up

All new bears arriving at the centre are quarantined for thirty days – this means they are kept apart from other bears at the centre. But cubs spend even more time in the quarantine area away from adult bears who might threaten or frighten them. During this time, Dr Wong checks they are healthy and will be safe to join the other bears.

Within days of arrival, bears are given a full medical check-up so that Dr Wong can judge whether they need any special care. They are looked after by a vet. The vet uses a tranquillising dart to put the bears to sleep so they can be safely moved. First, it's Tan-Tan's turn. Tan-Tan flinches but she flops as the tranquilliser hits its mark and is soon fast asleep. The Bear Care Crew roll the furry cub gently onto a sling to hold her steady.

Dr Wong watches intently as the vet examines Tan-Tan's sharp teeth and long, floppy tongue. She is weighed and her curved claws are counted on her big paws. Like our fingerprints, each sun bear's paws are unique. The vet uses a giant ink pad to take the bears' paw prints.

Baby Tan-Tan's paw print is labelled – she is Bear 44. When Kitud and Boboi arrive, they have their paw prints taken too and become Bear 45 and Bear 46.

Tan-Tan

Kitud

Boboi

Becoming best bear friends

In the wild, sun bears live alone with their mother, but this new home is just bursting with bears. Each bear holds a sad story inside. But company can bring comfort to lonely little bears.

In the rainforest, bears leave their scent by rubbing against trees. In this quiet way they keep their distance while still letting other bears know where they live. But these three cubs are keen for company . . .

At first Tan-Tan, Boboi and Kitud are nervous and shy as they are moved into separate enclosures in the Bear House. But they are curious because each is, in fact, a very bold little bear. After a few months Kitud and Boboi are moved next door to Tan-Tan so the three bears can touch, sniff and watch each other, but they can't yet play.

Finally they meet! The three bears are introduced and the wrestling begins immediately. Dark bundles of fur rush and roll and push and scramble. They learn from each other. Instincts kick in. They behave like wild bears. They are no longer full of fear – they are just full of fun!

Watching nearby, the Bear Care Crew relax. They put down the fire hoses, fire extinguishers and whistles that they had picked up in case of emergency. They were prepared for the bears to fight – they know that introducing bears to each other can go seriously wrong. But these cubs instantly create an inseparable bond. Boboi is bigger but Kitud is bolder. She leads the adventures with Tan-Tan close behind.

But Dr Wong wonders, *will they remember the smell of the forest, the warmth of the Sun and the sounds of the wild when they step beyond the Bear House?*

Zip-zap!

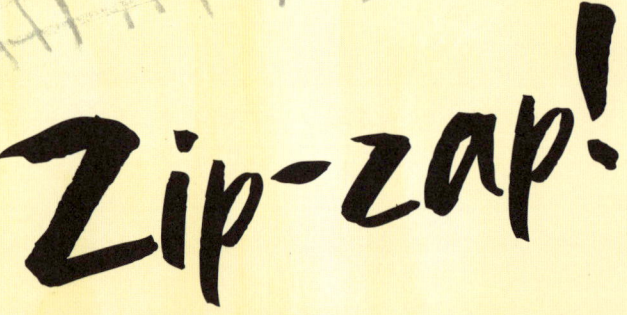

Before the three bears can be released back into the wild, they must face a test that will make them jump . . .

Sun bears in the Bear House are separated from the wilderness by a tall fence to keep them safe from predators, including humans. As rescued bears, they lack the skills needed to survive beyond the Bear House walls, such as knowing how and where to make a nest to sleep, how to forage for food and where to sleep to keep safe from pythons and leopards on the forest floor.

The fence is tall and pulses with solar-powered electricity to warn bears not to climb up and try to escape. Before bears are allowed into the fenced Forest Enclosure, for their own safety they must learn to be scared of the fence. The bear keepers are also scared of the fence . . . if a tree falls onto it, bears could escape. The keepers must quickly mend it to keep the bears safe.

One by one, Kitud, Tan-Tan and Boboi learn to be wary of the electric fence. Within twenty days they each pass this training test so the bigger, wilder Forest Enclose now awaits!

Forests full of life

The world's only populations of sun bears live in remote Southeast Asian forests outside the safety of the Forest Enclosure. In the rainforest, warm rain cascades from the canopy, splashing off leaves into tiny pools. Drops glide down the feathers of brightly coloured hornbill birds and slither down the sleek fur of sleeping sun bears, slumped in the trees. Every living thing in this humid habitat relies on the wealth of food and opportunities for life that the rainforest brings.

But this tangled forest is being cut down for palm oil groves that stretch to the horizon. Palm oil is used in many products, from toothpaste, shampoo and soap, to ice cream and pizza dough. What remains is a precious forest bursting with life. Thousands of different species of trees flourish as well as many orchids, animals, insects and the world's largest flower, which is more than a metre across. The 'corpse flower' attracts pollinating insects with its smell of rotting flesh.

**On the island of
Borneo, there are . . .**

3000 species of trees

300 species of reptiles

420 species of birds

In this extraordinary tangle of biodiversity, clouded leopards prowl, brightly coloured birds chatter, deadly pit vipers lurk and pythons slither. Pygmy elephants push through curtains of dark green leaves. High up, orangutans swing past wild sun bears resting in the trees.

Will our bears be ready to join them in this exciting, lush landscape soon?

15,000 species of plants

394 species of fish

222 species of mammals

Part Two:

Seeing the sky and smelling the earth

At last, the three little bears are ready to step beyond the enclosure for a short visit into the wild forest where they belong. But the cubs are nervous. They do not know that their soft paws should pad on soil or that their long, curved claws will help them climb trees. Lured by honey and tasty treats, they must be brave enough to venture down a ramp into the forest beyond. Tentatively, they poke their noses out and tap the ground with their paws . . . who will be first?

A honeybee buzzes and Kitud's wide eyes follow it up towards the sky. The sky! She can hear the noises of the forest – of bees and the shrill orchestra of cicadas, grasshopper-like insects, rubbing their wings in unison. She becomes curious, because all bears are, and steps forwards.

Tan-Tan follows her lead, as always. But Boboi backs into the safety of his familiar concrete floor, before finally joining his friends. He stands up on two legs, his long back curved forwards towards a leaf fluttering in the hot breeze.

The gentle wind brings so many smells, revealing so much to explore! The cubs roll in the dust, scratch in the dirt for termites and stare up at the trees. They play until dusk finally falls then the three tired little bears clamber back up the ramp and fall asleep, together.

Bear
necessities

It's time for three little bears to discover their bear necessities … the skills they need to survive.

Tan-Tan was orphaned before her mother had a chance to teach her how to climb. She would have taught Tan-Tan to keep her head up to avoid danger, find a comfortable place to rest, make a nest to sleep in, and in the rainy season, keep warm and dry. So Tan-Tan discovers that she is a record-breaking tree climber all on her own! She is soon wrapping her long legs around tree trunks and gripping them with strong claws. In just ten days she is twisting on branches and snapping twigs to make a nest in the trees.

Sun bears have poor eyesight but a great sense of smell, especially where honey is concerned. The cubs strengthen their muscles play-fighting and scrambling over each other. In the Forest Enclosure, they find hammocks, ladders and tyres. Bear House volunteers stuff old fire hoses with food that's tricky to get out. They smear banana leaves with peanut butter but, best of all, they make fruit ice lollies that the cubs lick and rub over their hot fur coats to keep cool under the scorching Sun!

These play things are known as 'enrichment toys' as by playing with them, the cubs are learning skills they need to survive. They discover how to forage for food and defend themselves against predators . . . the bear necessities of life in the wild.

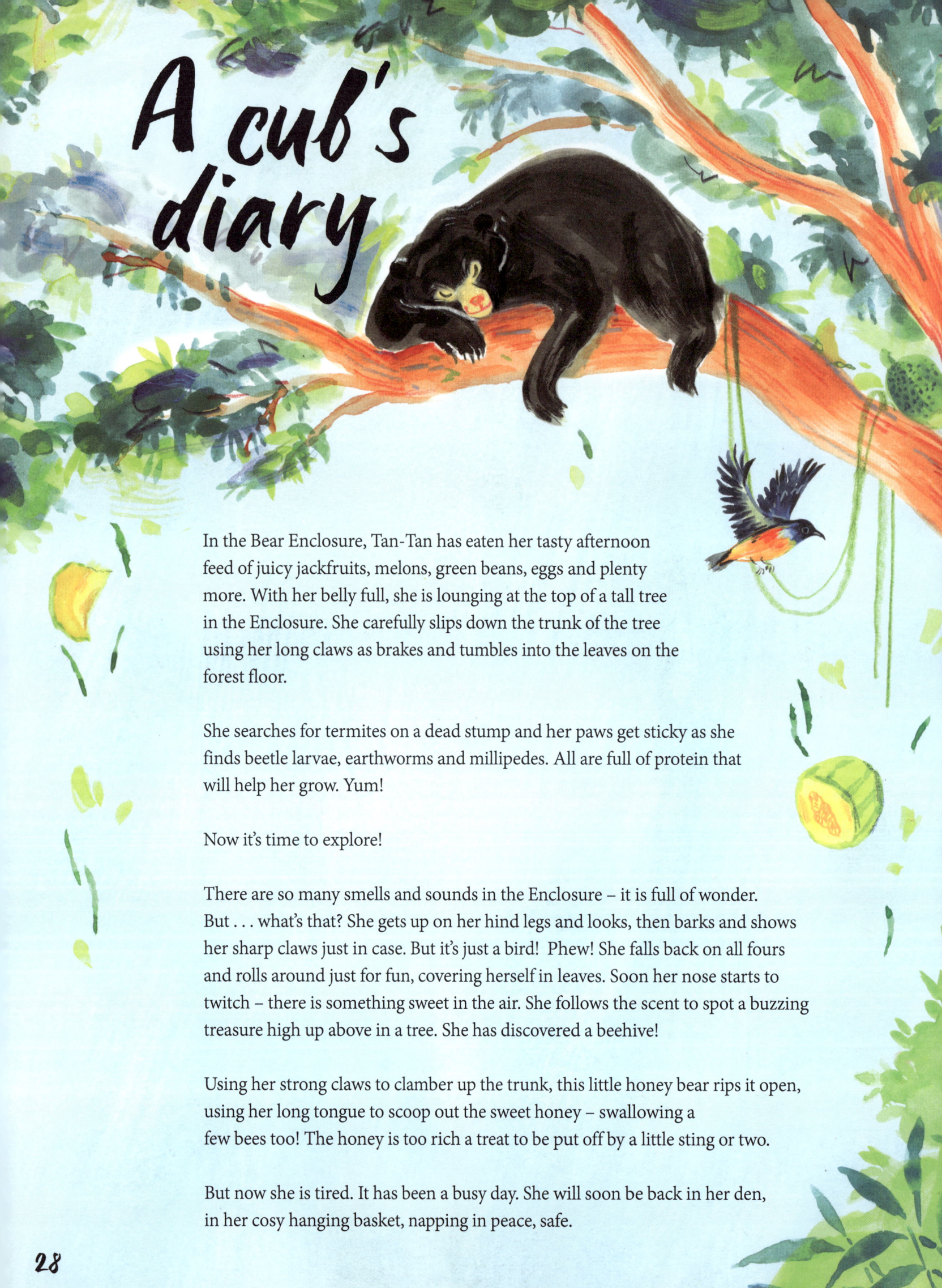

A cub's diary

In the Bear Enclosure, Tan-Tan has eaten her tasty afternoon feed of juicy jackfruits, melons, green beans, eggs and plenty more. With her belly full, she is lounging at the top of a tall tree in the Enclosure. She carefully slips down the trunk of the tree using her long claws as brakes and tumbles into the leaves on the forest floor.

She searches for termites on a dead stump and her paws get sticky as she finds beetle larvae, earthworms and millipedes. All are full of protein that will help her grow. Yum!

Now it's time to explore!

There are so many smells and sounds in the Enclosure – it is full of wonder. But . . . what's that? She gets up on her hind legs and looks, then barks and shows her sharp claws just in case. But it's just a bird! Phew! She falls back on all fours and rolls around just for fun, covering herself in leaves. Soon her nose starts to twitch – there is something sweet in the air. She follows the scent to spot a buzzing treasure high up above in a tree. She has discovered a beehive!

Using her strong claws to clamber up the trunk, this little honey bear rips it open, using her long tongue to scoop out the sweet honey – swallowing a few bees too! The honey is too rich a treat to be put off by a little sting or two.

But now she is tired. It has been a busy day. She will soon be back in her den, in her cosy hanging basket, napping in peace, safe.

Dr Wong's day

8 a.m. Check electric fence — make sure there are no holes or fallen trees

8:30 a.m. Chopping, slicing and peeling — food preparation for the bears' four meals a day

9 a.m. First feed in the Bear House
All the bears are checked to make sure they are healthy and happy

9:30 a.m. Bears are released into the Forest Enclosure. The Bear Crew clean up after these messy eaters

11 a.m. More food for hungry bears

1:30 p.m. Even more food for hungry bears!
The Bear Crew prepare activities for the bears

2 p.m. Dr Wong catches up with paperwork
Dens are mended, odd jobs are done

3 p.m. The Education Team guide school groups around the Centre

4 p.m. Bear dinner time!

6 p.m. Bears head back to their dens for the night

Walking with bears

Bear carers wear wellies and gloves because even little bears bite. Mostly the bears are just having fun but with those sharp teeth, it's best to be safe! In the forest, Kitud is adventurous. Boboi is cheeky and looking for fun. He stands tall on his hind legs to look around.

Tan-Tan is a caring little cub. She notices another bear who is always alone. She quietly moves closer and just sticks around.

These curious bears follow their Bear House guides deeper into the Forest Enclosure. They go further than they are brave enough to go alone and they stop to rest all together. Tan-Tan climbs trees and Kitud and Boboi tumble in the dust. All around, the forest is rich with smells and noisy with life. The three cubs smell the wild, unfenced rainforest beyond . . .

Mysterious giants...

a rainforest ecosystem

Deep in the rainforest, there is a very special tree. Sun bears and other wildlife depend on its fallen fruits – a bounty of food at different times of year, dotted throughout the forest. The special tree is a strangler fig. The fig tree is an important part of the network of living things that together make up this forest ecosystem.

Fig trees provide habitats for many species and a feast for forest life. Orangutans, gibbons and hornbills grasp its purple fruits high in the canopy. Deer, civet cats and rare Sumatran rhinoceroses pick fallen figs from the forest floor, while elephants stretch up for the juicy treats. In this food-rich habitat, sun bears also thrive.

These super trees, which may live as old as a thousand years, grow from a sticky seed carried on the fur of certain animals or in bird poo dropped from high in the canopy. It grows dangling roots that stretch down to the forest floor and eventually wrap around its host tree. These roots shade out the light above until the host tree dies and the fig tree stands solid and tall.

But these magnificent trees that sun bears and so many animals rely on are under threat, just like the sun bears that feed from them.

Instincts kick in

Dr Wong watches and waits to see if these little bears can survive on their own.

Back behind the Forest Enclosure's electric fence, he observes whether they find food and scamper up trees, and if they can build a nest. He is watching them relax and he even listens to them snore. Most of all, Dr Wong watches to see if they follow their natural instincts. He asks himself, *can they ever be wild bears again?*

It's a big question, because if he gets it wrong, these three little cubs that he has cared for will not survive. They must learn to be wary of people, to run from poachers who are sadly one of their greatest predators. To begin this six-month training of reduced human contact, this happy little bear cub trio are moved to the pens in the Forest Enclosure, far from visitors to the Bear House and far from human voices and human smells. They will not be allowed back to the Bear House at night – they must learn to survive on their own.

Tan-Tan, Kitud and Boboi pass the test with flying colours! They have faced so many challenges and overcome many fears but these brave bear cubs have proved they can survive in the wild. At last they will go back to the wilderness where they truly belong.

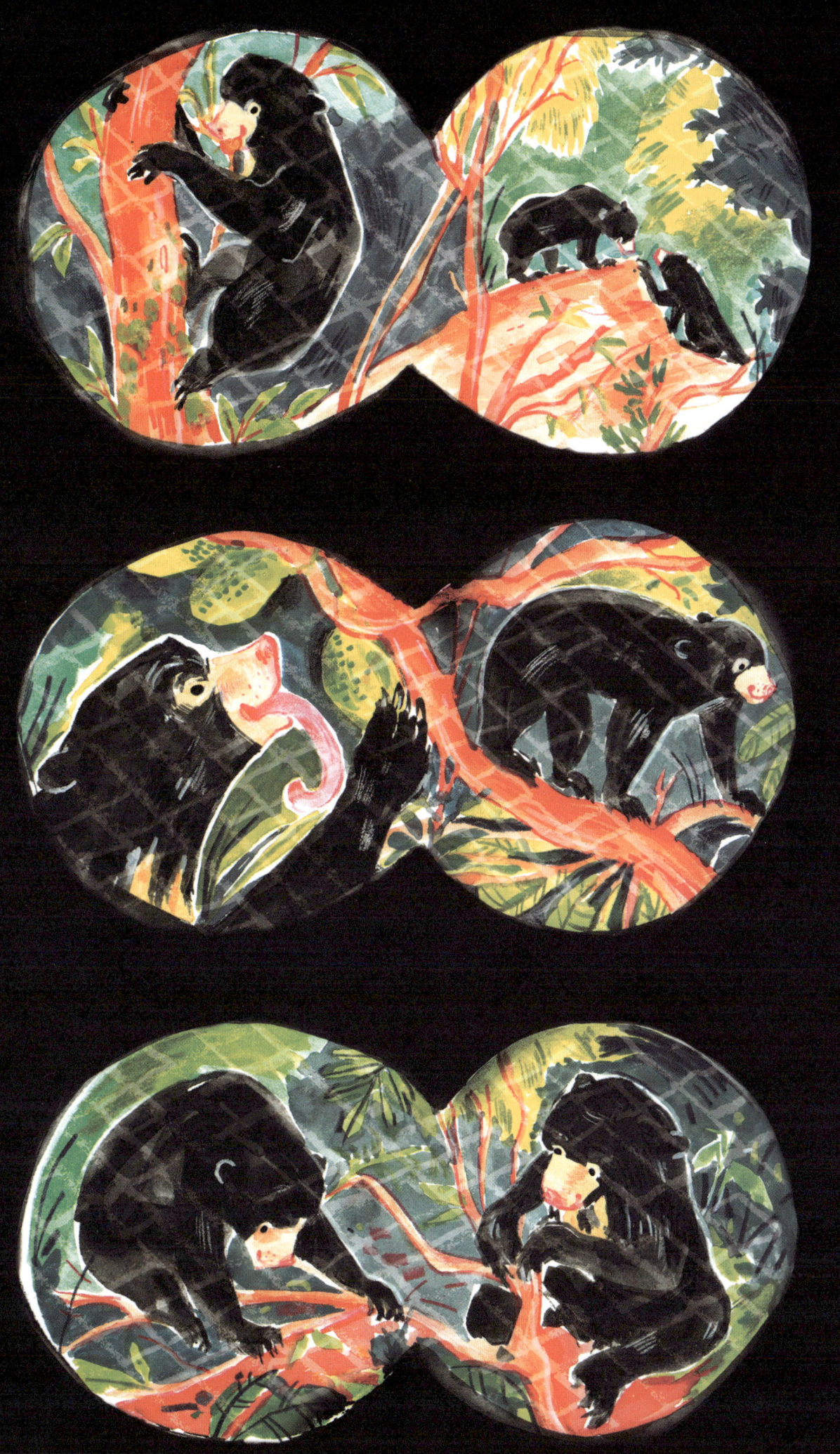

Countdown to
freedom

The big day has come . . . the rainforest awaits! It is four years since these little bears were rescued, just as in the wild they would have been four years old when their mother encouraged them to leave her side.

All three bears must have a final vet check-up before they begin their long journey back to the wild forest. Satellite collars are fitted so Dr Wong can keep track of them after they are released, however every time the collar gives a position, the battery will drop a little. So the more often you check, the faster the battery will run out. Dr Wong decides he will check twice a day so the battery should last about twelve months.

Never before has Dr Wong released three bears together to roam free. It is a big operation. And a big risk.

At 3 a.m. on 14 April 2019, it is dark. Dr Wong is nervous.
But he knows these brave little bears and his skilled team are
ready for this big bear move.

The sleepy, sedated bears are lifted into their metal crates,
cushioned by towels placed gently under their heavy heads.
As the Sun rises, they will wake slowly and need comfort
and also water. The truck stops where water floods the
road and the crates are carefully lowered into the
shallow flow, so the bears can cool off
and drink.

They drive north, passing palm oil
plantations that endlessly line the
road where forest once grew.

swing high

The Bear Team bump along dusty dirt roads into the heart of the remote Tabin Wildlife Reserve in north-east Sabah, Malaysia. It is Malaysia's biggest forest reserve, protected for its incredible diversity of rare plants, animals and fungi.

In the heart of this forest is a volcano that spews mud into a clearing where animals come to lick the salt and minerals found in the mud. It is the only open space in the dense forest where it is possible to land a helicopter far from the forest edge, the area where poachers may lurk.

The bear crates are lifted into a hammock below the helicopter, which swerves off swinging its heavy, furry load. Without a helicopter it would take three long, sweaty days to hack through the jungle to reach this place.

After twelve minutes, the pilot spirals down onto a gap in the forest the size of a football pitch. Here the air is thick with scent and sticky with heat, and ringing with the hoot of hornbills, singing gibbons and monkey chatter.

On other days tiny, hairy pygmy elephant calves slip and squelch with their mothers in the mud. But they're not here today – only footprints tell their tales. Today is all about bears.

Carrying Tan-Tan, Kitud and Boboi in their crates, the Bear Team are tense and exhausted, but excited.

Into the trees

Three crates, three bears . . . and a much wilder world beyond.

A rope is attached to the door of each crate so that it can be pulled open safely by the Bear Team, who are hidden behind nearby trees.

A countdown begins.

Dr Wong gives the command and with a tug, the crate doors slide open he three bears burst free! On their long legs, the three sun bears run back to the forest and straight up into the safety of the trees.

The Bear Team watch, different emotions pulling in different directions. The loss, the love and the relief.

But, most of all, they share hope.

With heavy but hopeful hearts, they lift the empty crates. As the helicopter blades whirr up to speed, they rise above the canopy. They look down and see nothing but trees. The three bears they loved are truly back where they belong. They hope they will never see them again, but that they will hear the radio collar bleeping as the cubs begin new, wilder lives.

Hidden journeys

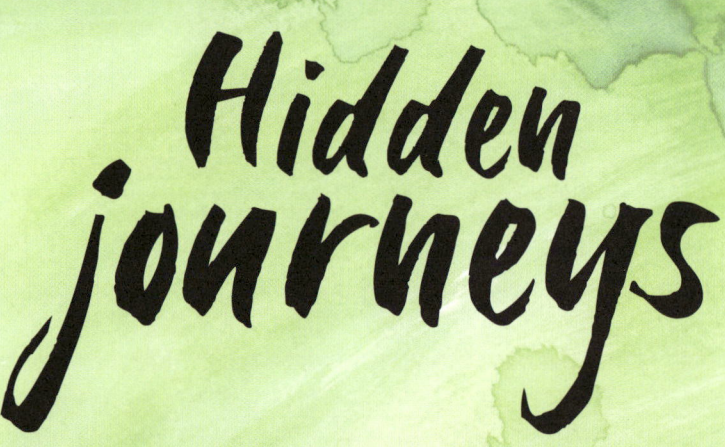

Tan-Tan, Boboi and Kitud were always the best of friends but now they must find their own way. In the wild, sun bears travel alone.

Anxiously monitoring their movements from their satellite collars, Dr Wong tracks them for a month and maps their journeys. They have each wandered deep into the forest, exploring in different directions. He worries how and where they will find food, which creatures they will meet and if these young cubs are scared without their mothers.

The collars of Tan-Tan, Boboi and Kitud fail after a month. It is not so unusual for radio collars to fail – sometimes the battery fails or runs out and sometimes collars just fall off. In this huge deep forest, it is impossible for Dr Wong to find out.

So, the travels of these three little bears beyond this map are a mystery. Once more, they are truly wild.

BEAR TRACKER MAP

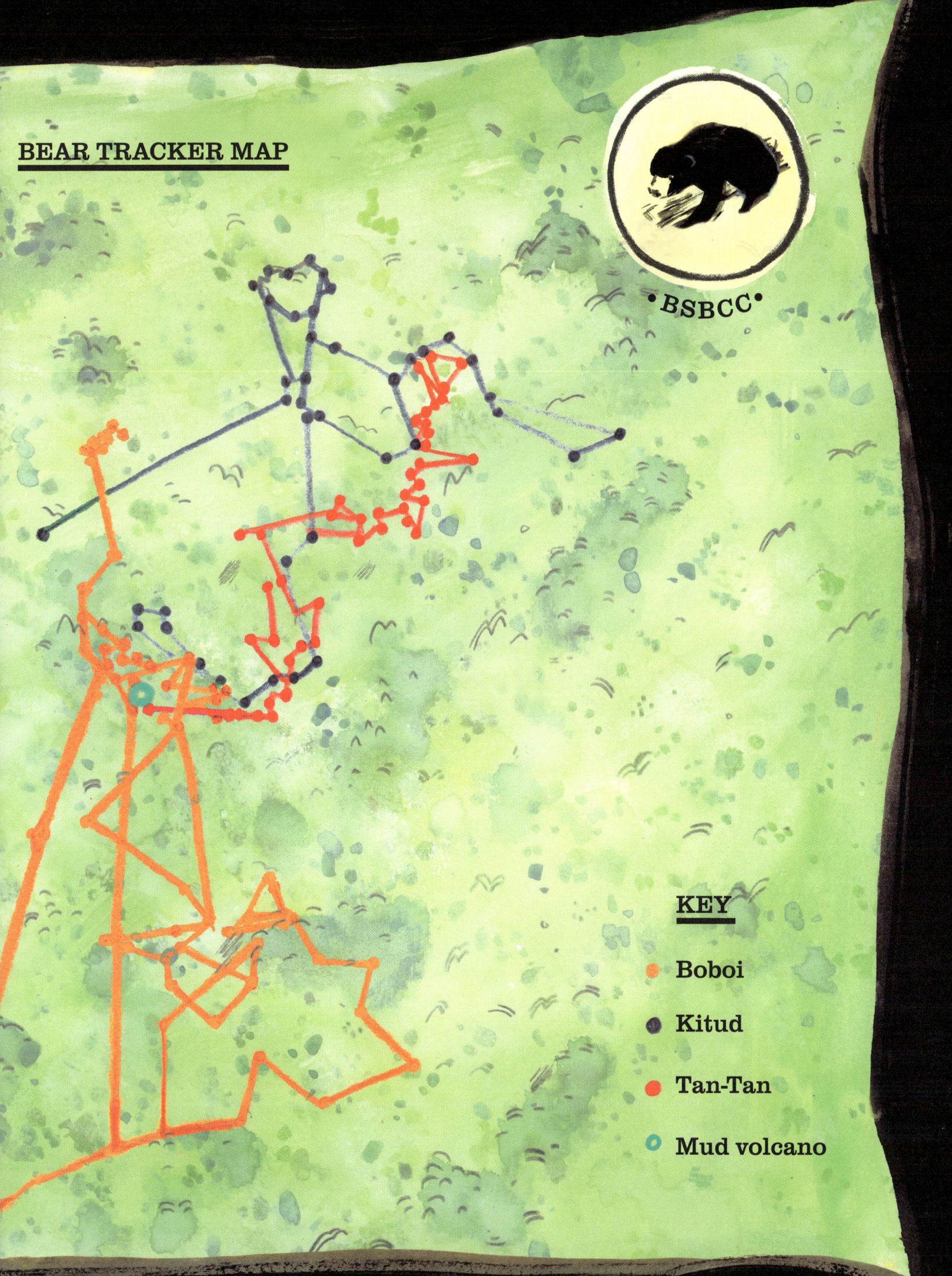

·BSBCC·

KEY

- Boboi
- Kitud
- Tan-Tan
- Mud volcano

Saving sun bears

Dr Wong and the Bear Care Crew hope their three little bears are safe. As you read this, the sun bears may have come together to gorge themselves on figs from the forest floor. Because when a magnificent strangling fig tree fruits, there is always more than enough for three.

No matter what, Tan-Tan, Kitud and Boboi are back in the wild – where all bears belong.

The Bornean Sun Bear Conservation Centre

Bornean Sun Bear
Conservation Centre

Island of
Borneo

The Bornean Sun Bear Conservation Centre (BSBCC) cares for rescued bears and shares their stories to inspire people all around the world to support them. The Centre carries out important research to help sun bear conservation. The team works with governments and local schools and supports ecotourism to raise awareness and understanding about sun bears and their precious forest habitats.

www.bsbcc.org.my

Working together, local people, indigenous communities who have always lived in these Bornean forests, scientists and campaigners around the world are determined to save rainforests, protect bears and stop the illegal wildlife trade. By sharing ideas, skills and information, they are saving sun bears.